MONDAY
abc NIGHT NFL
FOOTBALL
CLUB

NFL RULES!

Bloopers, Pranks, Upsets, and Touchdowns

PLAY
FOOTBALL
NFL

NFL RULES!
Bloopers, Pranks, Upsets, and Touchdowns

by JAMES BUCKLEY, JR.
& BRIAN PETERSON

Monday Night Football Club
Sections by Gordon Korman

HYPERION PAPERBACKS FOR CHILDREN
NEW YORK

ABC's *Monday Night Football* is a registered trademark of ABC Sports, Inc.

The National Football League, the NFL Shield logo, "NFL," "NFC," "AFC,"
and "Super Bowl" are trademarks of the National Football League. The NFL
team names, logos, helmets and uniform designs are trademarks of the teams
indicated.

Printed in the United States of America.
First Edition
1 3 5 7 9 10 8 6 4 2
This book is set in 12-point Caslon.

ISBN: 0-7868-1271-0
Library of Congress Catalog Card Number: 97-80387

Contents

Prologue

Three days to kickoff! thought Nick Lighter.

Three days to the start of a new season. The long months of no football were finally over. The preseason games had been great, of course. But the thrill of week one, the first step on the long road to Super Bowl XXXIII—there was nothing like it.

Super Bowl XXXII had been one of the greatest ever. The Denver Broncos had upset the Green Bay Packers in one of the most exciting big games of all time. Would the Broncos do it again this season? Would Green Bay come back? Nick couldn't wait to find out.

He had visions of football in every closet and corner. He punted his dirty socks into the laundry hamper. He took out the garbage by passing the bundled bags into the trash can. He couldn't even sit down on the couch without tackling the sofa cushions.

Being around his two fellow *Monday Night*

Football Club members only made things worse. When Coleman Galloway picked up the telephone, Nick pictured an opposing running back taking a handoff. Nick attacked like a linebacker on a blitz, grabbing and stripping. The receiver clattered to the floor.

"Fumble!" bellowed Nick.

He and Coleman both leaped for it. Elliot Rifkin threw himself into the fray.

"I've got it!" yelled Nick.

"No, *I've* got it!" cried Coleman and Elliot in unison.

As the fumbled phone was yanked back and forth, the cord wrapped around the lamp on the table.

Crash! The porcelain lamp hit the tiles and shattered.

"*What* is going on here?!"

Mrs. Lighter stood fuming at them.

"Nicky, have you lost your mind?" she demanded. "Look at my lamp!"

"Oh, that was my fault," Coleman explained. "I fumbled. Sorry."

"And I recovered," added Elliot, holding up the receiver. "Sorry."

"Hello? Hello?" came a tinny voice from the earpiece.

Coleman took the phone. "Oh, hi, Dad. I just wanted to remind you that the *Monday Night*

Football Club is at our house for week one."

The three held weekly sleepovers to watch *Monday Night Football* on TV.

Coleman frowned into the phone. "Really? The fifth time I told you? Are you sure, Dad? Dad?" He replaced the receiver. "I can't believe it. My own father hung up on me."

"Don't you see?" insisted Mrs. Lighter. "You're driving your families crazy with your football, football, football!"

"Well, excuse us for being psyched," Nick defended them.

This year, the *Monday Night Football* Club was doubly excited about opening day. For them, the new season meant another chance to use the Eskimos' shirt.

It was an old brown football jersey with an amazing secret. Anyone who fell asleep wearing it would somehow switch places with an NFL star. It had allowed Nick, Coleman, and Elliot to play in *Monday Night Football* games and even the Super Bowl. But the biggest thrill of all was to *be* John Elway, Barry Sanders, Dan Marino, Junior Seau, or Jerry Rice for a few precious hours.

"We'll calm down when the season starts," Elliot promised Mrs. Lighter. "Right now we're kind of suffering from football starvation."

"That's exactly why I bought you this." She handed Nick a thick paperback called *The*

Ultimate NFL Challenge. "It has a thousand and one questions. That should be enough football to keep even you three out of trouble until Labor Day."

"Answering a bunch of questions?" Nick said dubiously.

"Questions about football," she corrected. "It's going to work *or else*, Nicky. Is that clear?" And she gathered up the pieces of her broken lamp and stormed out.

"Thanks—I think," Nick called after her.

Elliot looked at the book in Nick's hands. "Well, it has to be sort of cool, right?" he offered. "I mean, it's the NFL."

"I guess." Nick flipped through the pages. "The problem is we know all this stuff. Look at this—'who's the number-one passer in NFL history?'"

Coleman snorted. "I could answer Dan Marino in my sleep. These questions are for average people, not total fans like us."

Nick frowned. "If only there was some way to make it harder."

Suddenly, Elliot snapped his fingers. "There is."

His two friends stared at him.

"The quiz is too easy by itself," Elliot explained. "But not when it's part of the Blind-folded Freewheeling Preseason Challenge Bomb."

Pranksville, U.S.A.

Elliot stretched the bandanna over Coleman's eyes and knotted it behind his head.

"This is impossible," Coleman complained. "How am I going to know where to pass if I can't see?"

"Let me worry about that," said Nick, lacing his Rollerblades. "Just make sure you don't throw it behind you." He stood up, wobbling on his wheels. "Okay, let's do it."

Quarterback Coleman got a grip on the football. Elliot clutched the quiz book. The Blindfolded Freewheeling Preseason Challenge Bomb was ready for kickoff.

Coleman barked, "Hut, hut, *hike!*"

Nick took off. He skated at top speed through Wigwam Park.

Coleman reared back and threw. The ball sailed high over the teepee fountain.

"Look out!" bellowed Elliot.

Nick swerved to avoid a seesaw.

He regained his balance just in time to hurdle a sleeping dog. He sneaked a glance over his shoulder.

Oh, no! The pass was headed right for the sandbox.

When his Rollerblades hit the sand, Nick had to run like mad to avoid falling on his face. At the last second he dove, throwing his arms out in front of him. The ball slapped into his hands just before he disappeared in a blizzard of sand.

Elliot scrambled through the tunnel of the jungle gym. He flung open *The Ultimate NFL Challenge* and read, "What star quarterback began his pro career with a haircut instead of a passing drill?"

Nick sat up, spitting sand and dabbing at a scraped elbow. "That's an easy one," he replied. "Picture this . . ."

Making the Cut

In the summer of 1993, rookie quarterback Drew Bledsoe was relaxing in his room at the Patriots' training camp. He was studying his playbook, getting ready to go to his first NFL practice. And he was really excited. This is what he had always dreamed of.

Drew had been the first choice of the Patriots in the NFL draft. He had his uniform, his playbook, and he had signed his first big contract. He had made it.

He was an NFL player.

Suddenly, the door burst open and a bunch of huge guys came rushing in. It's a little early to be avoiding tacklers, Drew thought—until he saw the scissors.

"Rookie haircut!" the veteran players shouted.

A few giant linemen held Drew down on the bed, while a couple more attacked his long hair with the scissors.

When they were done, Drew looked like he had lost a fight with a lawnmower.

"Welcome to the NFL, kid," the veterans said.

*　　*　　*

"That's nothing!" crowed Elliot, flipping through the book. "Get a load of these other great gags from training camp!"

*　　*　　*

I'll Get It

Jim Kelly was a great quarterback for the Bills until

he retired after the 1996 season. He also was a great joker.

When offensive tackle Ruben Brown was a rookie, Jim called him in to say that there was an important phone call.

"It's Mr. Wilson, the owner," Jim told Ruben. "You'd better hurry."

Ruben ran into the locker room, grabbed the phone . . . and got an earful of shaving cream, courtesy of his quarterback.

Thirsty?

Shawn King was a rookie defensive end with Carolina in 1995. During one training camp practice, he got a drink of water when he wasn't supposed to. The veterans took it easy on him, though: They tied him to the goalpost and turned a hose on him.

Walter the Baker

Walter Payton ran for an NFL-record 16,726 yards in 13 seasons with the Bears. He also made rookies run for cover.

A plate of donuts was a plate of pranks for Payton. He would slip in before the other players arrived and dip the glazed donuts in wax from the trainer's room. Then he would offer the yummy-looking treats to unsuspecting rookies.

The young players took one sticky, yucky bite, and immediately knew they had been fooled by a future Hall of Fame enshrinee.

Thirst-Aide

Coaches aren't much nicer to rookies. Bill Parcells has been a head coach in the NFL for 13 seasons with the Giants, Patriots, and Jets. At training camp before every one of those seasons, he appointed one rookie as his personal Gatorade-getter.

Drew Bledsoe (as if the haircut hadn't been bad enough!) was Parcells's chosen victim in 1993. Linebacker Willie McGinest was chosen in 1994. Cornerback Ty Law did the extra running in 1995. Linebacker James Farrior had the "honor" in 1996.

"Coach Parcells likes to drink that stuff a lot," Ty said. "Every time we took a break, I was running to the sidelines to get his Gatorade. And it had to be lemon-lime. No orange."

Jerry Worms

Once in a while, coaches themselves are victims of pranks. Jerry Burns was the head coach in Minnesota from 1986–1991. He was a good coach, tough and hard-nosed. But he hated snakes, worms, frogs, and other slimy things.

So, of course his players made sure he ran into creepy crawlies every chance they got. One of their favorite tricks was to put some worms in the coach's warm-up jacket while it hung in a closet. The team gathered around to watch him put on his jacket, stick his hands in his pockets . . . and freak out!

Staying on Their Toes

Not all training camp fun is aimed at rookies. A lot of the pranks are aimed at veterans.

When he was with the Raiders, quarterback Jeff Hostetler found some clear goop that had a secret side effect. He smeared the goop inside the shoes of some of his linemen. They didn't notice anything when they put their shoes on after practice.

But when they took their shoes off that night, their feet had turned blue!

Daily Oates

Bart Oates, who played on the offensive line for the Giants and 49ers from 1985–1995, discovered another use for something called DMSO. It is a liquid that is supposed to be rubbed on sore muscles. But it also has another effect.

Oates filled coach Johnny Parker's cologne bottle with the stuff. Coach Parker kept using his cologne, never knowing it wasn't what he had bought at the store.

A few weeks later, Oates knew his ploy had worked. DMSO had given Parker bad breath—really bad breath. Dog-slobber, sweaty-socks, onion-and-garlic bad breath. And for Bart, the best part was, Coach Parker didn't suspect a thing.

Oates not only was a Pro Bowl player, he also was an all-star prankster. He filled players' gloves with Vaseline. He snipped shoelaces. He hid clothes. He put eggs in helmets.

Oates was the ringleader when a bunch of Giants "kidnapped" rookie quarterback Dave Brown in 1992. They tied him up and dumped a bucket of kitchen garbage all over him.

2

Kickoff Classics

There were a few changes for the second try at the Blindfolded Freewheeling Preseason Challenge Bomb. Elliot switched to quarterback, and Nick took over *The Ultimate NFL Challenge*. This moved Coleman to wide receiver. But instead of Rollerblades, Coleman would have to make the catch while riding his little brother's old tricycle.

"Hut, hut, *hike!*"

Coleman pedaled like mad. The trike was so small that his high-pumping knees were knocking into his chin.

Then he saw the ball. The blindfolded Elliot had thrown far off to the left. The only way to get to it in time was . . .

"Cut through the playground!" bellowed Nick, running with the quiz book.

Coleman wheeled around, racing through

the teeter-totters. A hopscotch game scattered in front of him. The fleeing girls blocked his view. He never saw the swing set.

The canvas seat wrapped around his face. He was "clotheslined" off the tricycle.

Wham! He landed flat on his back on the grass.

The Blindfolded Freewheeling Preseason Challenge Bomb bounced off the teepee fountain. Like it was aimed by a friendly genie, it dropped right into Coleman's arms.

"I meant to do that," he called to Nick.

But Nick's head was buried in the quiz book. "What future Hall-of-Famer made NFL history in the first game of the 1994 season?"

"Everybody knows that," Coleman replied. "What a way to start the NFL's seventy-fifth anniversary season! It was 1994 . . ."

Rice's Record

Jerry Rice was playing his first game of the season. Everyone knew that the 49ers receiver would soon become the NFL's all-time leader in touchdowns scored. The only question was when he would break the record.

Rice wasted no time. He did it in the first *Monday Night Football* game of the season, when the 49ers played host to the Los Angeles Raiders.

Entering the game, Rice already had scored 124 touchdowns in his amazing career. Only Walter Payton and Jim Brown had scored more.

On the 49ers' fourth play from scrimmage, Jerry caught a pass over the middle from quarterback Steve Young. He broke a tackle, then all the Raiders saw was the back of his uniform. The 69-yard touchdown put Rice in a tie for second with Payton.

The 49ers were winning easily, leading 30–14 in the fourth quarter. San Francisco defensive end Dennis Brown made an interception that gave the 49ers the ball in Los Angeles territory. From the 23-yard line, the 49ers ran a reverse.

Young handed off to running back Ricky Watters. Rice sprinted around behind the line of scrimmage and got the handoff back from Watters. Then it was off to the races. The 23-yard score, the seventh rushing touchdown of Rice's career, tied him with Brown with 126 career touchdowns.

It looked as if Rice would have to wait another week to get the record. The 49ers were cruising and leading big. But there was a national audience watching . . . and waiting.

With just over four minutes remaining, Jerry broke free and headed for the end zone. Young's pass was a bit high, but Rice leaped, stretched, and outjumped two

Raiders defenders for a 38-yard touchdown.

When he came down with the ball, he was the NFL's all-time leading touchdown scorer. Rice has since become the all-time leader in receptions and receiving yards, too.

"Getting this record at home means a lot to me," Rice said after the game. "I'd like to give a game ball to every one of our fans."

* * *

Nick shook his head in admiration. "Something awesome always happens on opening day. Just look at these other unbelievable season kickoff games!"

* * *

The Dan and Drew Air Show

When two great passers face each other, fans expect fireworks—long bombs and bullet passes. They look for a high-scoring, high-flying, back and forth battle.

That's just what 71,000 fans at Miami's Joe Robbie Stadium got on opening day 1994.

New England's Drew Bledsoe and Miami's Dan

Marino are two of the NFL's best quarterbacks, and on that rainy afternoon in Florida, they put on an amazing air show.

Bledsoe completed 32 passes in 51 attempts for a club-record 421 yards. He threw 4 touchdown passes, including a 63-yard bomb to tight end Ben Coates.

Not bad for a passer in only his second season in the NFL.

But Dan Marino has been around for a while. Since that game in 1994, he has become the NFL's all-time leader in almost every major passing category. That day against the Patriots, he topped Drew's great numbers.

Dan completed 23 of 42 passes for 473 yards and 5 touchdowns. It was the eighteenth time in his career that he had thrown 4 or more touchdown passes, an NFL record. During the game, he surpassed 300 touchdown passes for his career, becoming only the second player ever to reach that number (Fran Tarkenton was the first).

Together, Marino and Bledsoe passed for 894 yards, the third highest total for two players in one game in NFL history.

Getting Off on the Right Foot

San Diego hadn't had much luck on opening days. Heading into their 1993 opener against Seattle, the

Chargers hadn't won the first game of a season since 1986.

John Carney kicked that losing streak right out of the stadium—along with everything else he touched that day. Carney kicked 6 field goals, scoring all of San Diego's points in the Chargers' 18–12 victory over the Seahawks. His club-record, field-goal total included kicks from 26, 44, 50, 32, 51, and 19 yards.

Flipper Football

The Dolphins visited the Chiefs to begin the 1972 season. The game was the first regular-season contest at Kansas City's new Arrowhead Stadium, but otherwise, it didn't seem like a big deal at the time.

In the first half, Dolphins quarterback Bob Griese threw a touchdown pass to Marlin Briscoe. Kicker Garo Yepremian booted a 47-yard field goal. And bulldozing running back Larry Csonka scored on a 2-yard run. At halftime, the score was 17–0.

The Dolphins scored only 3 points in the second half, but that would be enough. Their defense held the Chiefs to 10 points in a 20–10 victory.

So what was the big deal?

The opening-day victory was the first of 17 consecutive wins for Miami that season, the only perfect season in NFL history. The Dolphins won 14 regular-season games. They won two AFC playoff games. And they won Super Bowl VII, defeating Washington 14–7 in the Los Angeles Coliseum to close a history-making season.

The Saints Go Marching In...

When the Rams visited the New Orleans Saints on September 17, 1967, it wasn't just the Saints' first game of the season. It was their first game *ever*.

The Saints had joined the NFL that year, the first new team since Minnesota joined in 1961. New Orleans had a bunch of rookies and some veteran players chosen from other NFL teams, but they all were brand-new Saints.

One of the rookies was John Gilliam.

A speedy wide receiver from South Carolina State, Gilliam was sent back to receive the opening kickoff in the Saints' opening game. The Rams kicked off, and Gilliam caught the ball at the 6-yard line.

Zoom! He was gone!

He broke through the defense, hit the afterburners, and 94 yards later, he was in the end zone. The first play in Saints' history was a touchdown!

Still, they lost the game to the Rams 27–13. The

Saints lost 10 more games that season, finishing with a
3–11 record.

Opening-Day Surprise

When the Chicago Bears learned that they would be
opening their 1961 season against the Minnesota
Vikings in Metropolitan Stadium, they probably weren't
too worried.

The Bears were one of the oldest and most successful
NFL teams. They had been a member of the league
since it was founded in 1920. The Vikings were an
expansion team. This would be their first regular-season
game.

Not only that, but in the 1961 preseason, the
Vikings had lost five games by a combined score of
116–50. Stomping on the new kids on the block would
be a great way to start the season for the Bears.

Unfortunately for Chicago fans, the Bears weren't
playing very well. After the first quarter, Minnesota
led 3–0.

In the second quarter, Minnesota coach Norm Van
Brocklin switched quarterbacks. The coach put rookie
Fran Tarkenton into the game in place of George Shaw.
Suddenly, things changed.

The scrambling Tarkenton led the Vikings to the

biggest expansion-team upset ever. The underdog Vikings beat the Bears 37–13. Tarkenton passed for 4 touchdowns and ran for another.

The Bears were crushed—not to mention embarrassed. Not for long, however. The Vikings lost their next 7 games and finished 3–11. Chicago went 8–6, including a season-ending 52–35 victory over Minnesota.

A Record-Setting Opener

The only major single-game record that was set in a season-opening game came in 1951. And it has not been broken yet.

The Los Angeles Rams were hosting the New York Yankees (yes, there used to be an NFL team with that name) on a Friday night.

Bob Waterfield and Norm Van Brocklin alternated at quarterback for the Rams. Waterfield would lead the league in passing that year, with Van Brocklin finishing second.

Waterfield was injured that night, so Van Brocklin played the entire game.

Van Brocklin wasted no time in reaching the end zone. Shortly after the opening kickoff, he hit Elroy (Crazylegs) Hirsch with a touchdown pass. A few minutes later, the two teamed again. Then Van Brocklin hit another Rams receiver—Verda (Vitamin T) Smith—with a 60-yard bomb. And that was just in the first quarter!

By halftime, the Rams and Van Brocklin had a 34–7 lead. But the passing didn't stop there. Van Brocklin made the Yankees' defense look like Swiss cheese.

The Rams won 54–14. Van Brocklin completed 27 of his 41 attempts, and passed for 5 touchdowns, including 4 to Hirsch. The record? Van Brocklin passed for 554 yards that night in Los Angeles—still the most ever in one game by an NFL quarterback.

It was a good beginning to a great season. The Rams went on to win the 1951 NFL championship.

Bloopers, Part I:
The Bad Old Days

Elliot was next to take over the job of wide receiver. This time, the tricycle had been replaced by the Rifkins's wheelbarrow.

"Hut, hut, *hike!*"

Elliot sat in the wheelbarrow while Coleman pushed at a full sprint.

"Go right!" barked Elliot. He watched Nick's blindfolded pass sail over Wigwam Park. "Now—a little to the left . . . back to the middle . . . steady, here it comes—"

Elliot held out his hands to make the catch.

Whump! The wheel hit a rock. The barrow lurched to a stop. Instead of the ball, Coleman tumbled forward to land in Elliot's arms.

"Get out of here!" raged Elliot. "You're not the pass!"

Coleman reached up and pulled in the Blindfolded Freewheeling Preseason Challenge Bomb.

Nick sprang onto the scene. The bandanna was around his neck, the quiz book in his hand. "What NFL defensive end recovered a fumble and ran the wrong way?"

"I know!" chorused Coleman and Elliot.

"Hey," said Elliot. "It's *my* question. I'm the receiver."

Coleman held up the ball. "But *I* made the reception."

"Because my hands were busy saving *your* life," countered Elliot.

"I'll answer it," Nick laughed. "In 1964, Jim Marshall of the Minnesota Vikings had a great game—but that's not what anybody remembers. . . ."

Which Way to the End Zone?

The Vikings visited the 49ers in San Francisco on October 25, 1964. Vikings defensive end Jim Marshall was one of the fastest and best defensive linemen in the NFL. His coach, Norm Van Brocklin, called him "just about the fastest guy I ever saw [at that position]."

There were about seven minutes left in the first half, and the Vikings were ahead. George Mira went back to pass, but Jim Marshall, all 240 pounds of him, was bearing down on the quarterback. Mira tossed the ball downfield to receiver Bill Kilmer. Marshall changed directions and started after the ball. Kilmer was hit by two Vikings and fumbled.

Marshall picked up the ball and kept running, dreams of touchdown glory dancing in his head.

The problem was . . . he ran the wrong way.

Marshall was the only NFL player ever to be chased by his own teammates. The coaches and players on the sideline were going crazy! They waved their arms and shouted and pointed the other way.

Sixty-six yards later, Marshall crossed the goal line . . . the wrong one! He was so happy he'd made the run, he even tossed the ball away, out of the end zone.

That made it a safety for San Francisco, 2 points for the opposing team instead of 6 points for his team.

When he turned around and saw his teammates rushing toward him, he thought they were coming to congratulate him. Instead, they pointed out his mistake. Jim couldn't do anything but go back to the bench and hold his head in his hands.

But Marshall got over it quickly. His team won the game, after all, 27–22. He even joked that he should get paid by the 49ers because he played for them on one play.

*   *   *

Coleman elbowed Elliot, laughing. "Sounds like something you would do! Hey, Nick, maybe you should listen to this part . . ."

Remember Where You Play

In the NFL, everyone has a specialty. Each player has a position and skills that are important to playing that spot. Quarterbacks pass, linebackers tackle, running backs carry the ball, punters punt, and kickers kick.

Pretty simple, right?

Well, because one player forgot that simple rule, he created one of the biggest Super Bowl bloopers ever.

Garo Yepremian was the kicker for the Miami Dolphins. He was a good kicker, finishing third in the AFC with 115 points in 1972. He helped the Dolphins win 16 consecutive games to earn a spot in Super Bowl VII.

Yepremian had grown up in Cyprus, an island near Greece. He had played soccer as a kid, and didn't know anything about passing—just kicking.

In Super Bowl VII, the Dolphins' defense was awesome. Miami shut out the Redskins for nearly 58 minutes, and the Dolphins led 14–0. Quarterback Bob Griese had thrown a 28-yard touchdown pass to Howard Twilley, and running back Jim Kiick had scored on a 1-yard run.

With about 5 minutes left, Miami safety Jake Scott,

who was named the game's most valuable player, intercepted a Redskins' pass in the end zone and returned it 55 yards. A few plays later, the Dolphins decided to attempt a 42-yard field goal. In came Yepremian.

He lined up to try the field goal that would have made the score 17–0 for a 17–0 team. In a little more than two minutes, the Dolphins would become the only undefeated, untied team in league history.

Yepremian watched the snap hit holder Earl Morrall's hands. It was a bit low, but Morrall got the ball set up. The little left-footed kicker stepped forward and smacked the ball as hard as he could toward the goal posts at the front of the end zone (that's where the goal posts were in those days). But the kick was low and Washington's Bill Brundige blocked the ball back toward Yepremian and Morrall. It rolled around on the ground for a second.

Then Yepremian did something very strange.

He picked up the ball.

"I thought I saw some white jerseys downfield," he said later. "And that's why I decided to throw the ball. But it just slipped out of my fingers."

The ball went from Yepremian's slippery fingers right into the sure hands of Washington defensive back Mike Bass, who carried the worst pass in Super

Garo's goof

Dolphins kicker Garo Yepremian is about to attempt the silliest pass in Super Bowl history.

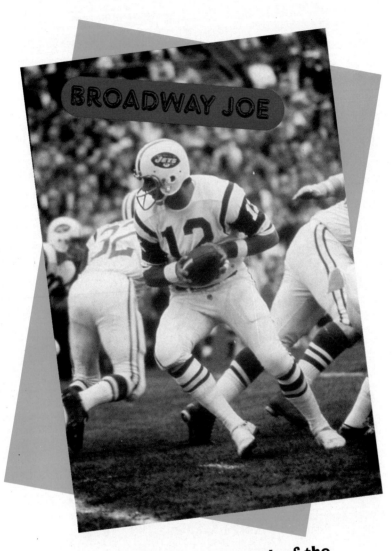

BROADWAY JOE

A confident Joe Namath of the New York Jets "guaranteed" a victory in Super Bowl III.

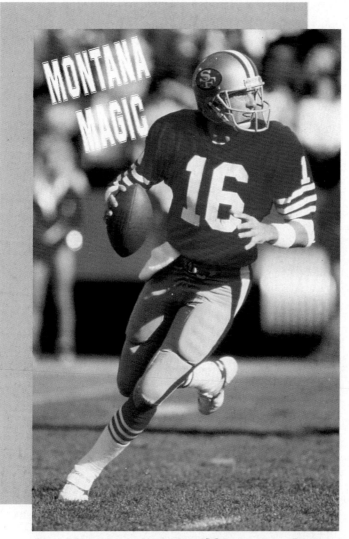

Joe Montana led the 49ers to a Super Bowl XXIII victory after a last-minute touchdown drive.

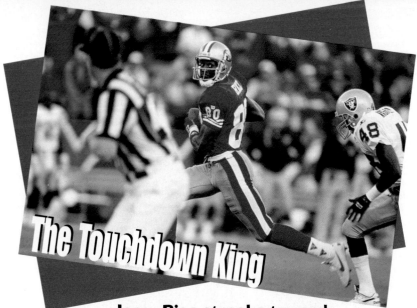

The Touchdown King

**Jerry Rice streaks toward
the end zone on his way to tying the
NFL's all-time touchdown record.**

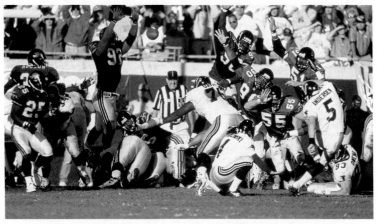

**Falcons kicker Morten Andersen (5) slips
and the Jaguars go to the playoffs.**

Is it an earthquake?

No, it's William "The Refrigerator" Perry
spiking a football into the turf during
Super Bowl XX.

Go, Bo, go!

Bo Jackson tore off on one of the greatest runs in Monday Night Football history.

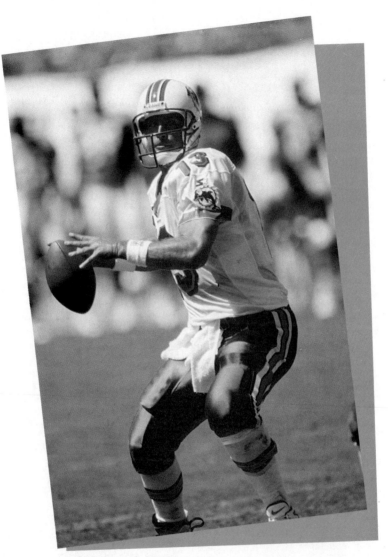

NFL legend Dan Marino gets ready to throw one of his perfect spirals.

Comeback King

John Elway finally got to hold up the Vince Lombardi Trophy after the Broncos won Super Bowl XXXII.

Bowl history 49 yards for a Redskins' touchdown.

Yepremian's pass was so bad, so awkward, so goofy, that it wasn't even ruled a pass. The NFL officially said he had fumbled.

"I've got to work with Garo," Griese said after Miami had wrapped up the 14–7 triumph and the Super Bowl title. "His throwing technique isn't what it should be."

All Fall Down

In 1978, the Giants forgot that when the game is nearly over, and your team is winning—fall on the ball.

The Giants weren't that good in 1978. In fact, the Giants hadn't been good for a while, with five losing seasons in a row. But on November 19, 1978, their record stood at 5–6. Not great, but not bad. Better still, the scoreboard read New York 17, Philadelphia 12. If they won this game, the Giants would be 6–6 and back in the playoff race.

To make things even more perfect, about 30 seconds remained in the game, and the Giants had the ball. All they had to do was run one play, and the game would be over.

Assistant coach Bob Gibson called a simple play, Pro-Up-65. But it wasn't simple enough.

"Usually when the quarterback is going to fall on the

ball," Giants center Jim Clack said after the game, "we tell the linemen to take it easy and not bury him. But when [Eagles defensive tackle] Charlie Johnson asked if he should take it easy, I said, 'No, we're running a play.'"

Quarterback Joe Pisarcik took the snap from Clack, and tried to hand the ball to fullback Larry Csonka.

It glanced off the running back's hip, bounced once on the artificial turf, and went right into the hands of an onrushing Herman Edwards, an Eagles cornerback. He took the gift and ran 26 yards untouched to the end zone.

Final score: Philadelphia 19, New York 17.

"They'll be talking about that play forty years from now," Edwards said. So far, he's right . . . it has been 20 years, and to NFL fans that play will always be known simply as "the Fumble"—a lesson in how *not* to end a game.

Coach Gibson was fired the next day. The team's general manager resigned. And New York's head coach left soon after. Pisarcik never did anything else in his NFL career to make people forget "the Fumble." Csonka managed to redeem himself. He later was elected to the Pro Football Hall of Fame.

Upsetmania

Nick skateboarded through Wigwam Park, kicking madly at the pavement for speed. Quarterback Elliot had gotten off the throw of his life. It would take a miracle for Nick to get to the ball in time.

He peered over his shoulder. The Blindfolded Freewheeling Preseason Challenge Bomb seemed to be headed all the way to the soccer field. The park patrol truck was stopped there while the maintenance man emptied out the recycling barrel.

Nick watched the long pass land right in the load of cans, bottles, and newspapers. Excited, he aimed his skateboard for the truck. Until the ball touched the ground, the play was still alive. That was the *Monday Night Football Club* rule.

The maintenance man got into the pickup. The engine roared to life.

Nick streaked in from behind. "Hey, Mister! You've got my ball!"

But the man didn't hear him. He put the truck in gear and started down the paved path.

Suddenly, Coleman ran out in front of the pickup, waving his arms. "Hey! No! Stop!"

The driver slammed on the brakes, and the truck screeched to a halt. Out of the flatbed popped a few plastic bottles and a football.

Nick hurled himself off the skateboard in a swan dive. He gathered in the ball a split second before he hit the pavement.

Elliot burst onto the scene with *The Ultimate NFL Challenge.* "What was the biggest upset in Super Bowl history?"

Nick rolled over and groaned. "Piece of cake," he replied. "It was Super Bowl III . . ."

*   *   *

Broadway Joe

When quarterback Joe Namath of the AFL's New York Jets "guaranteed" a victory over the NFL's Baltimore Colts in Super Bowl III, was Broadway Joe trying to hide his own worries? Or was Joe just very confident?

The 1968 Colts, one of the greatest pro football

teams of all time, were supposed to defeat the Jets. The previous two AFL teams had lost to the NFL-champion Green Bay Packers in Super Bowls I and II. Kansas City and Oakland had been defeated by 25 and 19 points. It didn't seem as if New York had much of a chance.

The Jets did have a few secret weapons beside the confident and flashy Namath. Head coach Weeb Ewbank had coached Baltimore to NFL titles in 1958 and 1959. Wide receiver Don Maynard was a future Hall-of-Fame enshrinee, but he was hurting, so George Sauer, the AFL's second-leading receiver in 1968 was the designated receiver that day with Maynard playing decoy. Kicker Jim Turner led the AFL in scoring in 1968, and running back Matt Snell was a big, bruising ball carrier.

New York showed the world it meant business from the start of Super Bowl III. On the second play, Namath called a sweep for Snell, who took the handoff, and barreled around the left side. He ran over Colts safety Rick Volk and picked up a first down. The Jets later were forced to punt, but Baltimore was rattled by Snell's power.

The first time the Colts got the ball, they advanced to the New York 19. But receiver Willie Richardson dropped a "sure" touchdown pass, and kicker Lou Michaels missed a 27-yard field-goal attempt.

On the second play of the second quarter things began to change. Jets cornerback Randy Beverly intercepted a pass in the end zone from Colts quarterback Earl Morrall. New York started from the 20, and barreled down the field. With 9:03 left in the first half, Snell scored on a 4-yard touchdown run, completing a 12-play, 80-yard drive.

New York took a lead that it never surrendered. The rest of the Jets' points came on 3 field goals by Turner. The Colts scored a touchdown near the end of the game, but New York's stunning 16–7 victory never was in doubt. Snell ran for 121 yards on 30 carries. Sauer caught 8 passes for 133 yards.

Namath's prediction may have seemed preposterous at the time, but it turned out to be right. The Jets' victory gave instant credibility to the AFL, which officially merged with the NFL in 1970.

*　　*　　*

Elliot waved the quiz book around like a signal flare. "Wow, I had forgotten some of these! Let me tell you guys about some of the other greatest upsets of all time."

*　　*　　*

The New Kids

The Jacksonville Jaguars and the Carolina Panthers could be considered modern-day versions of the 1968 Jets. Expansion teams always had struggled in their first few years in the NFL. For example:

- It took the Tampa Bay Buccaneers 26 tries before they won their first regular-season game.
- The Dallas Cowboys won only 25 games in their first 6 NFL seasons, including an 0–11–1 record in their first year.
- The Minnesota Vikings are the only expansion team ever to win their first game—a 37–13 surprise of the Bears. But they won a total of only 10 games in their first 3 seasons.
- The Seattle Seahawks managed a winning season in their third year.

Who would have thought the Panthers and Jaguars, both of whom entered the league in 1995, could do better?

Carolina exceeded all expectations in its first season. The Panthers won 7 games, the most ever by an expansion team. They also pulled off a shocking 13–7 upset of the San Francisco 49ers.

Entering week 10 of the 1995 NFL season, Carolina had won 3 consecutive games after losing its first 5 games. But the Panthers' winning streak was in trouble.

Next up were the 49ers, who had defeated the San Diego Chargers 49–26 in Super Bowl XXIX. One of the NFL's most successful franchises, the 49ers had won 11 division titles and at least 10 games per season every year since 1983.

San Francisco opened the game by driving 52 yards to Carolina's 38. But Panthers veteran linebacker Sam Mills forced tight end Brent Jones to fumble, and Carolina recovered the ball. Rookie quarterback Kerry Collins completed 3 clutch passes on the Panthers' first drive, which ended with a 39-yard field goal by John Kasay.

San Francisco answered the Panthers' score by moving the ball to the Carolina 7. Then lightning struck. Panthers cornerback Tim McKyer, formerly of the 49ers, intercepted a pass by Elvis Grbac, the backup quarterback who was playing in place of injured Steve Young, and returned it 96 yards for a touchdown. Carolina had a 12–0 lead.

Even superstar receiver Jerry Rice had problems with the upstarts from Carolina. On third-and-2 at the Panthers' 12 early in the second quarter, Rice caught a short pass and dashed for the end zone. Scoring touchdowns was almost second nature for Rice, the NFL's all-time touchdown leader. But, on this play, rookie cornerback Tyrone Poole punched the ball out of Rice's hands just before he reached the end zone. The ball went through the back of the end zone for a touchback.

The Panthers' defense played the key role in the victory. It forced 5 turnovers by the 49ers, including 3 when San Francisco was inside the Panthers' 3-yard line. The game marked the first time in NFL history in which an expansion team defeated a defending Super Bowl champion.

"It seems like one of the more improbable things, to come in as a rookie and beat the world champions," Collins said.

More New Kids

Jacksonville posted 4 victories in 1995, but made an even bigger impact in 1996. The Jaguars finished the 1996 regular season with a 9–7 record and earned a wild-card playoff berth. The Buffalo Bills never had lost a playoff game at home when the Jaguars went to Buffalo for an AFC Wild Card game. The Bills were expected to win. Just making the postseason had been an amazing feat for the second-year Jaguars.

But the Jaguars weren't satisfied just to be participating. They wanted to win.

The Bills opened the scoring on a 7-yard touchdown run by running back Thurman Thomas. Jacksonville struggled to move the ball early in the game. The momentum turned in the Jaguars' favor when defensive end Clyde Simmons intercepted a pass from Jim Kelly. He returned it 20 yards for a touchdown to tie the game at 7–7.

Thomas scored his second touchdown with a little more than two minutes left in the first quarter. Then it was running back Natrone Means's turn to grab the spotlight. Means's 62-yard run near the end of the first quarter set up a field goal, and his 30-yard touchdown rumble gave Jacksonville a 17–14 lead.

The score was tied late in the fourth quarter when Jaguars quarterback Mark Brunell completed 14- and 11-yard passes. That drive ended with the game-winning 45-yard field goal by kicker Mike Hollis. Jacksonville had a surprising 30–27 victory.

"They seem like the team we used to be," Bills Pro Bowl center Kent Hull said. "They made the plays when they had to have them. That's the reason they won."

Denver was the Jaguars' next opponent. The Broncos were the AFC's most dominant team in 1996 and had wrapped up home-field advantage throughout the play-offs by the thirteenth game of the regular season. A Jacksonville victory at Mile High Stadium seemed highly unlikely.

The Broncos led 12–0 at the end of the first quarter. The Jaguars appeared to be no match for mighty Denver. But Means stole the show again. He had runs of 18, 21, 13, and 17 yards, helping Jacksonville to score 23 unanswered points. They had a 23–12 lead with less than 11 minutes left in the game.

The NFL's comeback king, quarterback John Elway, tried to bring the Broncos back, but his effort fell short. Brunell's 18-yard touchdown pass to wide receiver Jimmy Smith with less than four minutes left sealed the Jaguars' 30–27 victory. Means carried the ball 21 times for 140 yards and a touchdown.

In the AFC Championship Game against New England at Foxboro Stadium, the Jaguars' Cinderella season came to an end, 20–6.

Comeback Kings

In the newest version of the Blindfolded Freewheeling Preseason Challenge Bomb, Nick was pushing Coleman in a pink polka-dot baby buggy.

"Come on!" urged Coleman. "Faster!"

Nick ran harder. But his foot struck a tree root, and he fell. The baby buggy continued to pick up speed down the gently sloping path.

"That's the way!" cheered Coleman from the baby buggy. "We're flying now!"

He had no idea that Nick was gone, and he was all alone on a runaway baby buggy. "Okay, Nick, you have to turn me around so I can make the catch. Ready? Turn!"

There was no answer. Wind whistled through the lacy frills of the seat cushion.

"Turn!" Coleman repeated. "I said turn! Come on, Nick! Nick?"

He looked over his shoulder. Instead of Nick, he saw the Blindfolded Freewheeling

Preseason Challenge Bomb screaming toward his nose.

"Aaaaah!"

Desperately, Coleman threw up his arms to protect his face. The ball slapped neatly into his hands. The force of the catch knocked him over. He and the baby buggy rolled across the grass, coming to rest in a patch of petunias.

And there was Elliot with the quiz book. "Name the NFL's top comeback king."

Coleman grinned, massaging a twisted knee. "That's a trick question. There are three players who are so awesome that it's impossible to choose among them. . . ."

Montana's Magic

Joe Montana was a third-round draft pick by the 49ers in 1979. In his second NFL season, San Francisco trailed New Orleans 35–7 at halftime. The 49ers needed a miracle, and Montana gave them one.

He began the second half by rushing for a 1-yard touchdown. He followed that score with a 71-yard bomb to wide receiver Dwight Clark to cut the lead to 35–21.

As the fourth quarter began, the Saints were sweating. What seemed like a sure victory was turning into a nightmare. Early in the quarter, Montana hit receiver

Freddie Solomon with a 14-yard touchdown strike. San Francisco trailed 35–28. When 49ers running back Lenvil Elliot scored on a 7-yard run with 1 minute 50 seconds remaining, New Orleans and San Francisco were tied.

The game went into overtime, and the 49ers won on a 36-yard field goal by Ray Wersching. The Saints were in shock. Montana had led the greatest regular-season comeback in NFL history.

In 1993, Montana joined the Kansas City Chiefs. They traveled to Denver for a big Monday night matchup with the division-rival Broncos on October 17, 1994.

The game was a seesaw affair. Through the first 3 quarters Denver and Kansas City each scored 3 touchdowns, including 2 scoring passes each by Montana and Elway. The Chiefs kicked a field goal early in the fourth quarter, but Elway responded by rushing for a touchdown with only 1 minute 29 seconds left in the game.

Denver led 28–24, but Elway had left too much time on the clock for Montana. So Montana coolly led Kansas City on a 9-play, 75-yard drive. It ended with a 5-yard touchdown pass from Montana to wide receiver Willie Davis with 8 seconds left. The 31–28 victory ended the Chiefs' 11-game losing streak at Mile High Stadium.

"You don't like to be in that situation too many

times," said Montana. "But that's all part of the game. It's nerve-wracking, but it's fun."

John's Number One

Montana may have gotten the best of Elway on that Monday night, but Elway is the NFL's all-time leader when it comes to rescuing his team in the fourth quarter. Entering the 1997 NFL season, Elway had guided Denver to 41 fourth-quarter comebacks (40 victories and a tie). Dan Marino of the Dolphins is second with 32, and Montana is third with 31.

Elway came to Denver in a 1983 draft-day trade after being picked first overall by the Baltimore Colts.

In 1986, Elway led the Broncos to their first AFC Championship Game in nine seasons. Denver was playing the Browns on a dreary day in Cleveland's Municipal Stadium.

The Browns took a 20–13 lead with 5 minutes left to play. On the kickoff, the Broncos messed up the return and ended up with the ball on their 2-yard line. Elway would have to take Denver 98 yards for a touchdown in less than five minutes just to tie the score.

"We've got these guys right where we want them," Elway told his teammates in the huddle as they stood in their own end zone.

As Elway began marching the Broncos down the field on what became known as "the Drive," Browns fans couldn't believe their eyes. Elway ran. Then he passed. He made long runs and short throws. He completed deep passes and eluded an angry pass rush. He did all of this while playing with a twisted ankle.

With 39 seconds to play, the Broncos faced a third-and-1 situation at Cleveland's 5-yard line. Elway called the play "Release 66." Broncos wide receiver Mark Jackson cut across the field and hung onto Elway's bullet pass for the game-tying touchdown.

In overtime, Elway completed 22- and 28-yard passes to position Rich Karlis for the winning 33-yard field goal, and Denver was headed to Super Bowl XXI.

"I remember thinking before the game that great quarterbacks make great plays in great games," Elway said. "That's what it's all about, isn't it? Until I can do that, I can't be considered a great quarterback."

Dan's Your Man

Dolphins quarterback Dan Marino, who was drafted the same year as Elway, is another NFL legend. Marino is the league's all-time passing leader in attempts, completions, yards, and touchdown passes.

There isn't a defense in football (except Miami's)

that wants to see Marino and his perfectly thrown spirals on the field in the closing minutes of a game. The New York Jets have been the victims of five fourth-quarter comebacks by Marino.

The last time was in November, 1994. The Jets, playing at home, dominated the first half, taking a 10–0 lead. Marino, who struggled in the first half, came to life in the third quarter when he threw 2 touchdown passes to wide receiver Mark Ingram. Miami cut New York's 24–6 lead to 24–14 heading into the fourth quarter.

Nearly 5 minutes into the fourth quarter, Marino again found Ingram for a 28-year scoring pass to cut New York's lead to 3 points. The Jets' defense dug in and tried to slow Marino's momentum. But with 2 minutes 34 seconds to play, the Dolphins got the ball back at their 16-yard line. Seven completions later, Marino had lifted the Dolphins to a 28–24 victory.

The touchdown pass that gave Miami the victory didn't even look as if it would be a play. Marino had moved Miami to the Jets' 8-yard line. With 30 seconds and no time-outs remaining, he hurried the offense to the line of scrimmage and motioned as if he was going to spike the ball to stop the clock.

The Jets—and almost everyone watching the game—also thought Marino would spike the ball.

Ingram knew otherwise. When Marino took the snap, Ingram darted toward the end zone, stopped, and looked back at Marino, who zipped him the ball. The stunned Jets saw Ingram catch his fourth touchdown pass of the game, giving Miami a 28–24 victory.

* * *

"But," challenged Coleman, "do you guys know who pulled off the greatest comeback of them all?"

* * *

Miracle in Buffalo

Although Montana, Elway, and Marino have been part of many comebacks, none of them was present for the greatest comeback in NFL history. It happened after the 1992 season during an AFC Wild Card Playoff Game between Houston and Buffalo at Rich Stadium.

The Oilers took charge early. They had a 35–3 lead after safety Bubba McDowell returned an interception 58 yards for a touchdown at the start of the third quarter.

Things looked especially grim for the Bills, who had two Pro Bowl players, quarterback Jim Kelly and linebacker Cornelius Bennett, out of the game with injuries. Star running back Thurman Thomas and defensive end Bruce Smith were playing but also were banged up.

No NFL team ever had won a game after trailing by so many points. If the Bills were going to be AFC champions again, backup quarterback Frank Reich needed to have the game of his life. Reich had engineered the greatest comeback in college football history as a quarterback at the University of Maryland. But could he do it again in the NFL?

Bills running back Kenneth Davis started the comeback with a 1-yard touchdown run to cut the lead to 35–10. Then Reich connected with Don Beebe on a 38-yard scoring pass. Three more touchdown passes, all to wide receiver Andre Reed, followed Beebe's score. Amazingly, the game was tied 38–38 at the end of regulation.

After Oilers quarterback Warren Moon threw an interception in overtime, Bills kicker Steve Christie made a 32-yard field goal to give Buffalo a mind-boggling 41–38 victory.

"I always believed," Bills linebacker Darryl Talley said. "I was always taught that as long as there is time on the clock, you never give up."

Bloopers, Part II:
The Book of Whoops

Elliot pedalled his bike between the rows of park benches. Behind him, he towed Coleman in a bright red wagon.

Nick launched a bad pass. The ball took off at a sharp angle to the right, sailing toward the jungle gym.

"Tu-u-urn!" cried Coleman.

Elliot wheeled around suddenly. The bike made the sharp curve but the wagon didn't. It flipped over, sending Coleman rolling across the grass. He finally came to rest in the dirt at the base of the big slide.

"Oof!"

A young boy shot down the slope, landing heavily on Coleman's stomach.

"Oof! Oof!"

Two more little kids bounced off.

"Hey, cut it out!" Coleman complained.

"But there's a meteor up there!" quavered one girl.

"A *meteor*?" echoed Coleman.

And then the "meteor" rolled down the slide and plopped right into Coleman's lap— their football.

Nick ran up, quiz book at the ready. "What superstar lost a touchdown for his team because he didn't have his pants on?"

Rubbing his poor bruised stomach, Coleman was grinning, ready with the answer. "Ah . . . that would be Desmond Howard. . . ."

When Dirty Play Is Okay

A football player needs a lot of equipment to play a game: helmets, shoes, pads, jerseys, and more. But forgetful players have misplaced their helmets, left mouthguards behind on the bench, and dropped gloves.

Desmond Howard really topped them all.

He forgot his pants.

Well, he didn't actually forget them. He was changing them. But he didn't do it fast enough, and it cost his team a touchdown.

Howard was the ace kick returner for the Green Bay Packers in 1996. He had a league-leading 3 touchdowns on punt returns in the regular season, helping the Packers reach an NFC Divisional Playoff Game against San Francisco.

Lambeau Field in Green Bay was very muddy for the

game, the result of rain all week long. The grass was slippery, and players were just standing in mud puddles on part of the field.

But a little mud never stopped NFL players.

In the first half of that game, Howard scored on a 71-yard punt return on which he eluded seven 49ers tacklers. The touchdown helped give Green Bay a 21–7 halftime lead.

Although he didn't get dirty on his touchdown run, he returned other kicks in the first half on which he was tackled. He also played some at wide receiver. So Howard, like his teammates, was a muddy mess as he headed into the locker room.

To make sure he wouldn't fumble the slippery ball off a muddy uniform, Howard changed into a clean jersey in the locker room. While he was at it, he thought, why not change his pants, too?

Whether he couldn't pull them on over his cleats, or whether he had trouble with the buttons, Howard wasn't with his teammates when they went back onto the field for the second half.

And he wasn't waiting where he should have been: on the goal line ready to receive the 49ers' kickoff to begin the second half. Unable to find their ace return man, Packers coaches sent in Don Beebe as an emergency replacement for the tardy Howard.

Beebe muffed the kickoff, the 49ers recovered on the 4-yard line, and scored a few plays later.

All because Howard wanted clean pants.

*   *   *

The *Monday Night Football* Club was rolling on the grass, helpless with laughter. "That's just the beginning!" gasped Nick. "Here are some bloopers that will blow your mind!"

*   *   *

Unlucky Leon

Leon Lett was enjoying every minute of Super Bowl XXVII. His team, the Dallas Cowboys, was romping over the Buffalo Bills. The Cowboys were on their way to the first of three Super Bowls they would win in four seasons.

A rookie defensive tackle, Lett was drafted out of Emporia State in Kansas, but he hadn't played much during the 1992 season, which led up to Super Bowl XXVII.

When the Cowboys built a big lead in Super Bowl

XXVII, Leon got more playing time. It was just the right opportunity for a young player to make a name for himself.

With 8 minutes remaining in the game, Dallas's Jim Jeffcoat sacked Buffalo quarterback Frank Reich. As Reich fell, the ball bounced out of his hands.

Leon was there to pounce on the ball at the Dallas 36. A huge field of green was ahead of him, and the end zone was in his sights. He took off with the ball tucked in the crook of his arm. He chugged away toward the goal line while the crowd in the Rose Bowl cheered.

It was a defensive lineman's dream come true. Not only was he on a winning Super Bowl team, he also was going to score a touchdown!

As he crossed the 5-yard line, Lett began to celebrate. He spread his arms wide. He held the ball way out at the end of his right arm.

Suddenly, just before Lett crossed the goal line, the ball wasn't in his hand anymore. A stunned Leon watched the ball bounce away in front of him—and out of the end zone.

Buffalo wide receiver Don Beebe had not given up when Leon began his run downfield. The speedy Beebe had sprinted after the big lineman and caught him. But there was no way the 183-pound Beebe would tackle the

295-pound Lett. So he did the next best thing.

He tackled the ball.

Leon helped, of course. By holding the ball out to the side, he let Beebe swat the ball away. It bounced through the end zone for a Buffalo touchback.

There was no touchdown for Lett, but he went away happy with a Super Bowl ring.

Morten Misses

Left-footed Morten Andersen of the Atlanta Falcons is one of the best kickers in NFL history. He has more 50-yard field goals than any other kicker, and has scored 1,641 points in 16 NFL seasons.

He is at his best from short range, as dependable as the sun coming up. From 1989 until the final play of 1996, he made 59 consecutive kicks from 30 yards or less.

But number 60 would be unlucky for Andersen, and the luckiest thing that ever happened to the Jacksonville Jaguars.

With just a few seconds remaining, the Jaguars led the Falcons 19–17. If they could hold on to the lead, they would qualify for a wild-card playoff spot. If they lost, their season was over.

It didn't look good for the Jaguars. With just four

seconds remaining, Andersen came in to try a 30-yard field goal. The Jaguars fans held their breath and hoped for the impossible.

Andersen's right foot planted into the turf and he slipped! His left foot hit the ball, but there was no chance. The kick sailed wide left, and the Jaguars sailed into the play-offs for the first time in their history.

Jacksonville players high-fived and jumped for joy. Their fans rocked the stands.

Andersen sat on the ground where he had landed and stared at the goal post.

Thanks to Andersen's blooper-reel kick, the Jaguars made the playoffs. Two remarkable wins later, they played in the AFC Championship Game, which they lost to New England 20–6. But they would have been home watching the playoffs on TV if it hadn't been for Morten's miss.

The veteran kicker took it all in stride—and with good humor. He even went back to Jacksonville in the offseason for the Jaguars' awards banquet. He presented the MVP trophy to quarterback Mark Brunell.

"I've learned a lot from that kick," Andersen said. "You can't take any kick for granted. You've got to really focus on every kick. I guess I didn't on that one."

Unbelievable Plays

"Be careful," Elliot called over his shoulder. "We've got to get this thing back to the supermarket in one piece."

He squatted in a wire grocery cart while Nick pushed him past the fountain.

"You want speed or safety?" snapped Nick. "Coleman got off a great throw."

Nick turned on the jets. But the Blindfolded Freewheeling Preseason Challenge Bomb sailed high over their heads. They would be too late to make the reception.

Nick and Elliot watched in horror as the ball plummeted from the sky right in the opening of a baby carriage. It all happened so fast that the little girl pushing it didn't even notice.

Nick and Elliot waited for the crying. It didn't come.

"Oh, no!" Nick hissed in agony. "Elliot, we knocked out a baby!"

At that moment, the girl's brother rode his bike full speed into the carriage, sending it flying. Out tumbled a life-sized doll and a football.

"I'm telling!" screamed the girl. She gawked as Nick hurled himself bodily out of the grocery cart and caught the ball.

Then came Coleman, cheering and waving the quiz book. "Who threw the most famous pass in 49ers history?"

"That's kid stuff," Nick replied as he righted the carriage and placed the doll inside. "It was the 1981 NFC Championship Game . . ."

The Catch

In the 1981 NFC Championship Game against the favored Dallas Cowboys, Joe Montana and Dwight Clark teamed up for "the Catch." The magical play propelled San Francisco to its first Super Bowl.

The Cowboys had a 27–21 lead when Montana led the 49ers' offense onto the field at San Francisco's 11-yard line with 4 minutes 54 seconds left in the game. In the next 4 minutes, Montana guided San Francisco to Dallas's 6-yard line. On third-and-3 with 58 seconds to play, Montana called "Sprint Option Right" in the huddle.

At the line of scrimmage, Clark saw that he would be double teamed. He wasn't the primary receiver on the play. All he wanted to do was run a good pass route and be a decoy. When the ball was snapped, Clark ran toward the middle of the end zone.

Montana rolled right, chased by the Cowboys' fierce pass rush. Clark, seeing Montana in trouble, doubled back to the right along the back of the end zone.

A desperate Montana threw the ball as the Cowboys' Ed (Too Tall) Jones closed in on him. Clark jumped as high as he could, stretched his arms towards the sky, made a fingertip grab, then got both feet down in bounds. Clark's catch was the game-winning touchdown in the 49ers' 28–27 victory that gave San Francisco a berth in Super Bowl XVI. The 49ers defeated Cincinnati 26–21 for the first of their five Super Bowl victories.

"I knew Dwight had to be back there," Montana said. "He always was. But I sure couldn't see him. I jumped up and threw the ball and went down and rolled over. And then I heard the crowd! I knew the pass was high. Dwight must have jumped three feet to get it."

*   *   *

"They're not football players—they're magicians!" cried Coleman. "Listen to more of the most amazing plays in NFL history. . . ."

*   *   *

A Happy Return

When Green Bay's Desmond Howard got ready to receive New England's kickoff near the end of the third quarter in Super Bowl XXXI, the Patriots had just scored to cut the Packers' lead to 27–21.

The Packers, who were the NFL's most dominant team in 1996, suddenly looked beatable.

But it took Howard only 17 seconds to crush the Patriots' dreams of a Super Bowl victory.

The Packers' backup receiver, who had won the Heisman Trophy at the University of Michigan in 1991, caught Adam Vinatieri's kickoff at the 1-yard line and headed upfield. Howard's blockers on Green Bay's kick-off-return team set up a perfect wedge, like well-trained bodyguards protecting the star of the show. Howard jetted up the middle of the field and raced for a Super Bowl-record 99-yard touchdown.

Even the Jumbotron helped him on his return. Howard, who was named the game's most valuable player, looked up to the supersize scoreboard once he had broken into the clear. His score, and a 2-point conversion, gave Green Bay a 35–21 lead that it never surrendered in winning the NFL title.

"At about the 25-or 30-yard line," Howard said, "the wedge opened and I saw a lane to the left. I hit that hole. I did check the Jumbotron to see where the kicker was. I remembered that kicker running down [Dallas kick returner] Herschel Walker in one game. So I made sure [Don] Beebe blocked him, and I checked the screen."

With a Pass and a Prayer

Sometimes a little luck—or even a prayer—decides whether or not a play becomes a legend. The Dallas Cowboys trailed the Minnesota Vikings 14–10 with 1 minute 51 seconds remaining in a 1975 NFC Divisional Playoff Game at open-air Metropolitan Stadium.

The Cowboys had the ball on their 15 yard line. It took Dallas quarterback Roger Staubach 8 plays and 89 seconds to move his team to midfield. Then, on second down and 10 with 32 seconds to go, Staubach let go one of the most famous passes in NFL history. He took the snap, faked to his left, turned to his right, and launched a wobbly pass downfield.

Staubach had asked wide receiver Drew Pearson if he could run a deep corner pattern on first down. Pearson, who had just caught a pass, said he was too tired to try it again that soon. But on second down, Staubach called the same play. This time Pearson said he was ready.

Pearson battled for position with Vikings cornerback Nate Wright as the ball neared Minnesota's 5-yard line. Wright lost his balance and fell. Pearson caught the ball, but almost let it slip through his hands. After clutching the ball on his hip, Pearson gathered it to his chest and danced into the end zone. The Cowboys won 17–14 and were headed to the NFC Championship Game.

"I wound up, threw, and said a prayer," Staubach said. "It was just a Hail Mary pass . . . a very, very lucky play."

Pinball Wizard

Few plays in NFL history have generated as much controversy as a play that is known as "the Immaculate Reception." Did Terry Bradshaw's pass bounce like a pinball off Raiders defensive back Jack Tatum or Steelers running back John (Frenchy) Fuqua?

If it went off Tatum, the play was legal, and the ball could be caught by anyone. If it hit Fuqua first, the ball could be touched next only by a defensive player.

Whoever touched it first remains a mystery. Steelers running back Franco Harris, who was trailing the play, scooped up the deflected pass just before it hit the ground and made what became known as "the Immaculate Reception."

Until that day, Pittsburgh never had won a playoff game. The Steelers finished 11–3 in 1972 and were hoping to change their postseason luck in an AFC

Divisional Playoff Game at Three Rivers Stadium.

The game was a defensive struggle. With 22 seconds remaining, the Raiders led 7–6. The Steelers had the ball, but faced a fourth-and-10 at their 40. Bradshaw, a brash and confident quarterback from a small college, Louisiana Tech, stepped into the huddle and called "66 Option."

Bradshaw took the snap and was forced to roll right. He was hit just as he released the ball. Fuqua leaped high for the pass but collided with Tatum as the ball arrived. The ball caromed 15 yards backward, where Harris caught it off his shoe tops and ran for the game-winning points.

Fuqua approached Harris, who was in his rookie year and had been nicknamed Stallion by his teammates, at Harris's locker after the game. "Stallion, my man, my main man," Fuqua said. "You look . . . immaculate."

Monday Night Magic

Coleman rolled along the paved path in Mr. Galloway's black leather swivel chair. This was the best freewheeler of them all, he thought. He could zoom forward. But when the time came to make the catch, he simply would swivel back to face the ball. He just had to avoid the workmen who were setting up wooden boards to protect a newly planted garden.

The Blindfolded Freewheeling Preseason Challenge Bomb soared in a graceful arc overhead. Coleman timed his move carefully.

One . . . two . . . three! He spun around on the speeding chair.

Perfect! The ball was headed straight for him.

"Okay, Ralph," said one workman to his partner. "Coffee break."

Ralph set his sheet of plywood down against the edge of the fountain. The two men started walking away.

Rolling backward, Coleman shot up the

board as if it was a launching ramp. His terrified shriek echoed all around Wigwam Park. He and the swivel chair sailed high in the air.

Splash! They landed in the fountain.

The two workmen came running back. "Kid! Kid! What are you doing?"

Coleman bobbed up, choking and sputtering. He opened his stinging eyes just in time to see the ball. His diving catch dunked him under once more.

Nick and Elliot were laughing so hard they had to hold each other upright. Nick barely managed to choke out the question. "What *Monday Night Football* record might be tied, but will never be broken?"

"Wait a minute," said Ralph, the workman. "All records can be broken."

"Not this one . . ." gurgled a very wet Coleman.

Taking It to the Limit

An NFL field is 100 yards long, but a player can't have a 100-yard run from scrimmage because the ball has to start on the field, not in the end zone. So 99 yards is the maximum play from scrimmage.

Before the Monday night game between Dallas and Minnesota on January 3, 1983—the last game of the

1982 regular season—the longest run from scrimmage in NFL history was 97 yards by Andy Uram in 1939 and Bob Gage in 1949.

But after the Monday night game, a new name was in the record books—Dallas running back Tony Dorsett.

After the Vikings scored to take a 24–13 lead, they kicked off to Dallas's Timmy Newsome, who fumbled the ball out of bounds at the 1-yard line.

Taking a handoff from quarterback Danny White, Dorsett ran through a hole in the left side of the Vikings' line into the secondary. He outraced two more would-be tacklers and cut back across the field toward the right sideline.

He was going full speed as he crossed the 50-yard line, but two more Vikings were headed his way to cut him off. (It didn't help the Vikings to discover they only had 10 players on the field.) Suddenly, wide receiver Drew Pearson caught up with Dorsett, and got in the Vikings' way. Pearson's block allowed Dorsett to slip by. A few tightrope-walking steps down the sideline later, Dorsett was in the end zone and in the record book with the NFL's first 99-yard run.

After Dorsett finished his run and accepted congratulations from his teammates, he flipped the ball to one of the officials, who tossed it to a ball boy, who probably just put it back with the other balls being used in the game. That was the only mistake Dorsett made on his long run.

"I didn't realize it was a record until I got to the side-line," he said later. "Then the first thing I thought of was: I can't believe I didn't save the ball!"

*   *   *

"That's the total reason why we formed the club," said Coleman with a shrug. "If you miss *Monday Night Football*, you might as well watch bowling. Check out some of these other Monday night miracles. . . ."

*   *   *

Campbell Makes Dolphin Soup

The Monday night game on November 20, 1978, between Miami and Houston had a chance to be great. Both teams were headed for the playoffs. The Oilers' slogan was "love ya blue," and thousands of blue-and-white pompons had been given out for fans to shake. The partisan crowd's extra-loud cheers made the Astrodome shake.

"They were all waving those doggoned pom-poms," Oilers coach Bum Phillips remembered. "They were more into it than any game I've ever been a part of."

Houston running back Earl Campbell, the rookie who had won the Heisman Trophy at Texas the year before, put on one of the best *Monday Night Football* performances ever, gaining 199 yards and scoring 4 touchdowns.

His first score, a 1-yard run, came in the first quarter and tied the game 7–7. He scored again in the third quarter on a 6-yard sweep to the left side that gave Houston a 21–14 lead in an exciting, back-and-forth game that saw the score tied three times with three lead changes.

The fourth quarter, however, was when Campbell took over.

With Houston trailing 23–21, he took a pitch from quarterback Dan Pastorini and swept around the right end for a 12-yard touchdown.

Campbell capped the Oilers' big night with an electrifying 80-yard run up the right sideline. He sprinted around the right end, then just flat out beat any defender who tried to catch him from behind. It was an awesome sight—a 235-pound running back outracing speedy defensive backs.

The touchdown made the score 35–23. Miami came back with one more touchdown, but it wasn't enough to overcome Campbell.

Campbell gained 199 yards in the game to go over the 1,000-yard mark for the season and take over the NFL rushing lead. He would end up with 1,450 yards for the season and win the first of his 3 consecutive NFL rushing titles. He is now a member of the Pro Football Hall of Fame.

The Fridge Ices Green Bay

William Perry was an enormous rookie defensive end for the Chicago Bears in 1985. He stood 6 feet 4 inches and weighed 308 pounds, much of it in his very large belly. His nickname was "the Refrigerator," but everyone called him "the Fridge."

Perry made a name for himself against the Packers in a *Monday Night Football* game on October 21, 1985.

Three times in the first half of that game, which Chicago won 23–7, Bears coach Mike Ditka sent the Fridge into the game when Chicago had the ball near the Packers' goal line. Ditka also had sent Perry in twice the week before as a running back; the Fridge gained 4 yards in 2 carries.

With Chicago trailing 7–0, the Fridge was sent in on a goal-line situation. The Green Bay linebacker opposite him was George Cumby. At the snap, the 224-pound Cumby moved to fill a hole in the Green Bay line. The Fridge leveled him with a crunching block that allowed Walter Payton to score.

The next time, Perry carried the ball himself, bulling for a touchdown from the 1-yard line.

Later in the first half, the Fridge returned to blocking, clearing a monster-sized hole in the Green Bay line that paved the way for another touchdown by Payton.

"On my second touchdown, it felt like I was stealing," Payton said after the game. "He's great to hide behind."

On his own touchdown play, at the snap of the ball, the Fridge got all of his 308 pounds moving forward—a freight train in a football uniform. Quarterback Jim McMahon stuffed the ball into Perry's big gut.

The Fridge barreled into the end zone like, well, a refrigerator on wheels. He fired the ball into the turf with a humongous spike. A legend was born.

After the game, the Fridge was surrounded at his locker by a mob of reporters. The young player with the big stomach and the bigger smile answered all their questions.

"I was just having fun," he said.

Bo Knows Monday Night

Vincent Edward (Bo) Jackson was one of the fastest and strongest running backs ever to play in the NFL. Jackson also used his speed and strength to be an all-star baseball player with the Kansas City Royals.

In 1987, Jackson rushed for a *Monday Night Football* record 221 yards and scored 3 touchdowns as the Raiders routed the Seattle Seahawks 37–14.

His first touchdown of the night came on a 14-yard pass from Marc Wilson. It was Jackson's first NFL receiving touchdown, and made the score 14–7.

A few minutes later, Jackson added one of the best touchdown runs in Monday night history.

The Raiders were pinned deep, facing a third-and-6 from their 9-yard line.

It was time to call in Bo.

He took the handoff from Wilson and ran toward the left side of the Raiders' line. Jumping over diving Seattle safety Eugene Robinson, Jackson turned on the afterburners and outsprinted the entire Seattle team. On the replay, it looks as if Jackson was going full speed while everyone else was in super slow motion.

After he cruised through the end zone, Jackson just kept running, disappearing into a tunnel that led underneath the stands. When you're going that fast, it takes a while to slow down. Several Raiders teammates raced into the tunnel after him to congratulate him. Finally, a few moments later, Jackson, the ball, and the Raiders all came jogging out. The Seattle crowd was not very happy, but the Raiders fans watching *Monday Night Football* were psyched. The 91-yard run set a club record.

But Jackson wasn't finished. In the second half, he had a 42-yard run on a drive that led to his scoring on a 2-yard touchdown run. On that score, he bulldozed Seahawks linebacker Brian Bosworth.

At the end of the game, Jackson had rushed for 221 yards, a *Monday Night Football* record. The date of that classic game?

November 30, 1987 . . . Bo's twenty-fifth birthday.

Washington Goes Wild

On September 18, 1978, in the fourth quarter of a Monday night game played in a driving rainstorm in Foxboro, Massachusetts, Joe Washington went wild.

In only his second game with the Baltimore Colts, Washington threw a touchdown pass, caught a touchdown pass, and returned a kickoff for a touchdown. About the only things he didn't do were kick a field goal or sell popcorn in the stands.

Led by Washington, the Colts scored 27 points in the fourth quarter to win 34–27.

Washington had joined the Colts from the Chargers only two weeks before the game against the Patriots. He was so new to the team that he didn't even know most of the plays. Another player, usually fullback Roosevelt Leaks, would show Washington where he was supposed to go after the play was called in the huddle.

Trailing 13–7 entering the fourth quarter, the Colts let their new guy take over. First, Washington took a pitch from quarterback Bill Troup, rolled to the left and threw a 54-yard halfback-option pass to Roger Carr.

Then Washington was on the other end of a touchdown pass, this time a 23-yard effort from Troup. That gave Baltimore a 27–13 lead.

But the Patriots weren't done. They scored 2 touchdowns of their own and tied the score with 78 seconds left. But they forgot one thing. Or, rather, one player.

After New England tied the score, the Patriots' John Smith kicked off. The ball landed at about the 20-yard line and bounced around on the rain-slick artificial turf before skidding back toward the return man.

Unfortunately for New England, that return man was, at least for one night, Super Joe.

Behind a wall of blockers, and working hard to keep his footing on the slippery surface, Washington ran 90 yards for the game-winning touchdown.

It was another Monday night to remember.

Super Bowl Memories

"How are you enjoying the quiz book?" called Mrs. Lighter from the kitchen.

"It's pretty good," Nick called back.

To his friends he whispered, "Keep your mouths shut. If we tiptoe, we can sneak to my room without Mom seeing us."

Coleman took one step with his soaking-wet sneakers. *Squish!*

"What's that noise?" Mrs. Lighter poked her head through the doorway. She screamed at the sight of them.

The *Monday Night Football* Club was a spectacle to behold. Sand rained onto the floor from Nick's hair and clothes. Elliot was a mass of dirt clumps and grass stains. And Coleman looked as if he had just gone over Niagara Falls.

"Hi, Mom," Nick greeted her weakly. "Is that a new dress?"

"What *happened*?" she cried. "You were supposed to be answering quiz questions!"

"We were," Elliot explained sheepishly. "I

guess we got a little carried away."

"The NFL is so exciting that even a quiz can be pretty wild," added Coleman with a sneeze.

"You three are going straight into the shower!" thundered Mrs. Lighter. "Coleman, Elliot—I'm calling your mothers to come over with clean clothes."

"No!" blurted Elliot. "I mean, uh, please don't bother. I mean—" he hung his head. "I'm dead."

"Me, too," Coleman added mournfully. "And I think I'm getting a cold."

"You should have thought of that before you turned a simple quiz into World War III," scolded Mrs. Lighter.

They started down the hall.

"The worst part," muttered Nick, "is that we never got to the most important questions of all—the chapter on the Super Bowl."

"That's great stuff," Elliot agreed, flipping through the book. "Listen to this: who actually coined the name 'Super Bowl'?"

"Lamar Hunt, naturally," Coleman answered right away.

Super Inspiration

Kansas City Chiefs owner Lamar Hunt was the first person to call the championship game between the AFL and NFL the "Super Bowl." Hunt's inspiration for Super Bowl came from his kids. His wife had given their children super balls, which were made of dense rubber and could bounce as high as a house.

During a committee meeting following the AFL-NFL merger agreement in 1966, Hunt asked if there should be a week off before the championship game. Someone responded to Hunt's question by asking him which championship game he meant, the AFL or the NFL. Hunt responded by saying, "Well, I mean the final game, the last game, the Super Bowl."

"It just came out," he said. "The name of the ball must have been in my subconscious. It was just one of those spontaneous things."

*   *   *

Nick snatched the book from Elliot's hands. "Let's read the best of the best—the greatest moments from the Super Bowl."

*   *   *

Super Joe
In 1988, the 49ers struggled for much of the season,

and quarterback Joe Montana took the blame. San Francisco stumbled to a 6–5 record. Montana was in danger of losing his starting job.

But he rallied the 49ers to six victories in their last seven games—including playoff wins over Minnesota and Chicago—to advance to Super Bowl XXIII. There, San Francisco met Cincinnati in a rematch of Super Bowl XVI. The 49ers won that first meeting 26–21 in January, 1982.

Most of Super Bowl XXIII was a defensive struggle. Neither offense scored a touchdown in the first three quarters. The 49ers trailed 16–13 with 3 minutes 20 seconds remaining in the game when they got the ball on their 8-yard line.

There was tension in the air, but Montana *seemed* totally calm. In the huddle, he turned to tackle Harris Barton and playfully pointed out that actor John Candy was in the stands. But Montana was actually just hiding his nervousness well.

On the first play of the drive, Montana threw an 8-yard pass to running back Roger Craig. Montana completed 6 of his next 7 passes and moved the 49ers to the Bengals' 10-yard line. With 34 seconds left, Montana zipped a 10-yard touchdown pass to wide receiver John Taylor (his only reception of the day) to give San Francisco a dramatic 20–16 comeback victory.

"Joe Montana is not human," said Bengals receiver Cris Collinsworth, who played in both of Cincinnati's Super Bowl losses to Montana's 49ers. "I don't want to call him a god, but he's definitely somewhere in between."

Powerful Passers

Joe Montana isn't the only NFL quarterback to play his best in the Super Bowl. Giants quarterback Phil Simms completed a Super Bowl–record 88 percent (22 of 25) of his passes in New York's 39–20 victory over Denver in Super Bowl XXI.

The Broncos were victimized again in Super Bowl XXII when Redskins quarterback Doug Williams became almost superhuman, throwing 4 touchdown passes in one quarter. Denver had a 10–0 lead, but Washington scored 35 unanswered points in the second quarter and went on to win 42–10. "It was the greatest quarter of football I've ever seen," said Redskins head coach Joe Gibbs, who was inducted into the Pro Football Hall of Fame in 1996.

It was the greatest quarter *anyone* had ever seen in postseason NFL football.

In Super Bowl XXIX, 49ers quarterback Steve Young stepped out of Montana's shadow by throwing a record 6 touchdown passes as San Francisco scorched the San Diego Chargers 49–26.

Simms, Williams, and Young all were named most valuable players of their Super Bowls.

Run to Daylight

Ball carriers also have made a big impression in the Super Bowl. The Redskins' John Riggins, a big, bruising, speedy running back, was a force in Super Bowl XVII. His 43-yard touchdown run off left tackle on fourth-and-1 with Washington trailing 17–13 boosted the Redskins to a 27–17 victory over Miami.

"Riggins hurt," Dolphins safety Lyle Blackwood said. "When you hit him, it hurt."

In Super Bowl XVIII, Marcus Allen dazzled the crowd by reversing fields and setting off on a winding 74-yard touchdown run—the longest in Super Bowl history—that helped propel the Raiders to a 38–9 victory over the Redskins.

And who can forget the touchdown plunge of the mammoth Bears' defensive tackle turned running back, William (the Refrigerator) Perry, in Super Bowl XX?

The Greatest Super Bowl Ever

It took Denver Broncos quarterback John Elway four tries, but he finally got a Super Bowl ring. In arguably the best Super Bowl ever played, Denver defeated Green Bay 31-24 in Super Bowl XXXII in San Diego.

For the past 15 NFL seasons, Elway has been one of the league's best passers and a master of come-from-behind victories (see chapter 5). But he had never been able to win the big one. Elway had shouldered much of the load for his previous teams, which lacked a strong offense and defensive balance.

In Super Bowls XXI, XXII, and XXIV, the Broncos and Elway were defeated by scores of 39-20, 42-10, and 55-10, respectively. The week before Super Bowl XXXII, many people also predicted Denver would lose to the Packers by a large margin.

Super Bowl XXXII didn't start well for the Broncos. Green Bay drove 76 yards in only 8 plays on the opening drive of the game, scoring when quarterback Brett Favre teamed with wide receiver Antonio Freeman on a 22-yard touchdown pass.

Denver rebounded by scoring 2 touchdowns (1-yard runs by running back Terrell Davis and Elway) and a field goal on its next three drives to take a 17-7 lead.

Another touchdown pass by Favre cut the Broncos' lead to 17-14 just before halftime.

Green Bay tied the score 17-17 with a field goal on its first series of the second half, but Denver responded with another 1-yard scoring run by Davis near the end of the third quarter.

Favre threw his third touchdown pass of the game at the beginning of the fourth quarter, and the score was tired 24-24. Each team was forced to punt on its next two possessions.

The Broncos got the ball back with 3 minutes 27 seconds left in the game and drove 49 yards in 5 plays for the game-winning touchdown. The Packers had one final chance, but on fourth-and-6 at Denver's 31-yard line with 32 seconds remaining, Favre's pass for tight end Mark Chmura was broken up by linebacker John Mobley, sealing the Bronco's victory.

Despite missing the entire second quarter with a migraine headache, David rushed for 157 yards and 3 touchdowns and was named the game's Most Valuable Player. Elway didn't have a great passing game in Super Bowl XXXII—he completed only 12 of 22 passes for 123 yards and had 1 interception—but it didn't matter. He masterfully directed the Broncos' game plan and became an NFL champion.

Super Odds and Ends

Viewed by more than 140 million Americans each year, the Super Bowl is the biggest single-day sports spectacle in the world. Nine of the top 10 most watched programs in television history are Super Bowls. Super Bowl Sunday has become an unofficial national holiday.

The only Super Bowl that wasn't sold out was the first one between Green Bay and Kansas City at the Los Angeles Memorial Coliseum (the first two Super Bowls were called the AFL-NFL World Championship Game). Only 61,946 people attended in a stadium that seated 94,000. Super Bowl I was televised by both CBS and NBC—the only time two major networks shared the broadcast rights.

The highest priced ticket for Super Bowl I was $12, or about the amount it costs today for four packs of football trading cards. The best seats for Super Bowl XXXII cost more than $350.

Everything about the game has gotten bigger.

At Pepsi's Super Bowl XXVIII party, 18,000 slices of pizza were given away. The party goers also consumed 300,000 ounces of Pepsi, 3,000 pounds of ice, and 1,000 pounds of barbecue beef sandwiches.

At the Hyatt Regency in Atlanta, the host city for

Super Bowl XXVIII, 7,200 bottles of water, 10,000 bottles of assorted juices, and 85 racks of lamb were consumed on Super Sunday.

The winning Super Bowl team takes home the Vince Lombardi Trophy, named after the Green Bay Packers' legendary coach. It is made of sterling silver, stands 21 inches tall, and weighs 7 pounds and 3 ounces. Each trophy is worth $10,000.

Epilogue

Two hours later, not one of the three boys had been anywhere near the shower. By that time, the *Monday Night Football* Club had answered one thousand of the thousand and one questions in *The Ultimate NFL Challenge.*

Nick turned to the last page. "Remember, this is for our perfect score. What Super Bowl MVP bonked his head against the Lombardi trophy during a postgame interview?"

Coleman frowned. "Hey, wait a minute! That never happened!"

"No-o-o!" howled Nick.

Elliot stared at Coleman in disbelief. "You bonehead! How could you not know? You of all people!"

Coleman looked blank. "What are you talking about?"

"It was *you!*" cried Nick. "When you switched bodies with Dan Marino for the Super Bowl, you had trouble changing back. You had to conk yourself on the head to reverse the effect of the Eskimos' shirt!"

"Oh, yeah!" Coleman's wide-eyed face slowly rearranged itself into a crooked smile. "Cool! I made *The Ultimate NFL Challenge!*"

"The official answer is Dan Marino," Nick reminded him.

"Well, it was *his* head," Coleman admitted. "But *I* did the conking."

"You did a great job, too," snarled Elliot. "You must have scrambled your so-called brains. Coleman, you just cost us a perfect score on the quiz."

"I lived it," Coleman defended himself. "I shouldn't have to answer questions about it."

Nick cradled the book as if it were a million-dollar diamond necklace. "Man, the NFL has such an awesome history! And thanks to the Eskimos' shirt, we were a part of it!"

"Correction," said Elliot. "We *are* a part of it. And we'll keep on being a part of it—as long as we've got that sweater."

"Bring on the new season!" cheered Coleman. "The *Monday Night Football* Club is ready to rumble!"

FEEL THE POWER ON-LINE!

NFL.COM is the official website of the National Football League and the ultimate online destination for football fans. From late-breaking news to comprehensive team profiles to live scores and play-by-play every game day, NFL.COM covers it all. Fans can interact with their favorite players, sound off in polls and chat about the "big game."

And now there's a brand new section devoted to you—Play Football. Filled with fun games, stats, trivia, and more, Play Football is jam packed with all the information you need to impress your folks, astound your friends, or learn more about the game.

• **NFL News:** For the latest headlines, team standings, and scores.

• **Pro Stats:** Includes the season's stats leaders, all-time stats leaders, and the unexpected stat of the week. It's stat-sational!

• **Game Zone:** There's more than one way to Play Football in the Game Zone with "Quarterback Scramble," "Double Vision," "Soak the Coach," "Home Dome" and more!

• **You Make the Call:** It's your site. Tell us what you think with photo captions, polls, and fan feedback.

• **NFL Kids:** See what the NFL is doing for kids like you. Check out information on our youth programs, like how to join an *NFL Flag* league, or how to *Take a Player to School*.

• **NFL Teams:** Choose your favorite team to get team trivia, star players, history, and records.

Y FOOTBALL IS THE PLACE TO BE THIS SEASON, OFF-SEASON, NEXT SEASON, ANY SEASON! CHECK IT OUT TODAY.

NFL Flag
Presented by Nike

Do you want to play Flag Football? Well, the NFL has set up Flag leagues for you to join across the country including twenty NFL cities Arizona, Carolina, Chicago, Cincinnati, Dallas, Denver, Detroit, Green Bay, Jacksonville, Kansas City, Miami, New England, New Orleans, New York (2), Oakland, Philadelphia, Pittsburgh, San Diego, and Tampa Bay) in 1998. You must be between the ages of 6-14 years old. Join in the Spring and/or Fall.

NFL Gatorade Punt,
Pass & Kick

he largest NFL youth skills competition in sports is expanding to reach ore of you (boys and girls ages 8-15) through local in-school competitions nationwide. Test your ability to throw and kick a football as far d accurately as you can. If you win in your local school, you go on to e "Sectional" competition, from there it's to the "Club" division, and if you win there, you go all the way to the "National" championships. *Punt, Pass, & Kick* takes place throughout the month of September.

NFL C.I.T.Y. Football

NFL C.I.T.Y. Football brings backyard football to the cities. It includes instructional football sessions, followed by flag football games. Last ar, NFL C.I.T.Y. Football only took place in 5 NFL cities, but this year the NFL brings it to more of you. There are 20 cities involved this year Arizona, Carolina, Chicago, Cincinnati, Cleveland, Dallas, Denver, Detroit, Green Bay, Jacksonville, Kansas City, Miami, Minnesota, New England, w Orleans, New York (2), Oakland, Philadelphia, Pittsburgh, San Diego, n Francisco and Tampa Bay). *C.I.T.Y. Football* runs throughout the year d includes the following programs: Instructional Camps, Flag Leagues, and mentoring components.

For more information on how to become more involved in these programs, check out PLAY FOOTBALL on NFL.com

Get Amped for the X Games Xtreme Mysteries

Shred It Up This Spring

Available Now

X Games Xtreme Mysteries #1
Deep Powder, Deep Trouble
ISBN 0-7868-1284-2

X Games Xtreme Mysteries #2
Crossed Tracks
ISBN 0-7868-1281-8

Coming in June

X Games Xtreme Mysteries #3
Rocked Out: A Summer X Games
Special
ISBN 0-7868-1283-4

X Games Xtreme Mysteries #4
Half Pipe Rip-Off
ISBN 0-7868-1282-6

Every single book is jammed to the max with Xtras:

- full-color photo insert featuring action shots of a champion X Games
  athlete, his/her tips on safety, and a complete bio
- exclusive special offers
- player stats
- the X Games broadcast schedule
- plus much more